FAR HILLS

MOOSE-
MOUSE'S
HOUSE

PINEY WOODS

THE
FISHING STREAM

SHADEY GLEN

SWEET
MEADOW

UNCLE EZRA'S
SECRET PROJECT

THE
APPLE
ORCHARD

BIZZY &
EZRA'S
HOME

OLD STONE WALL

For Richard - J.B.M. For my family - S.O.

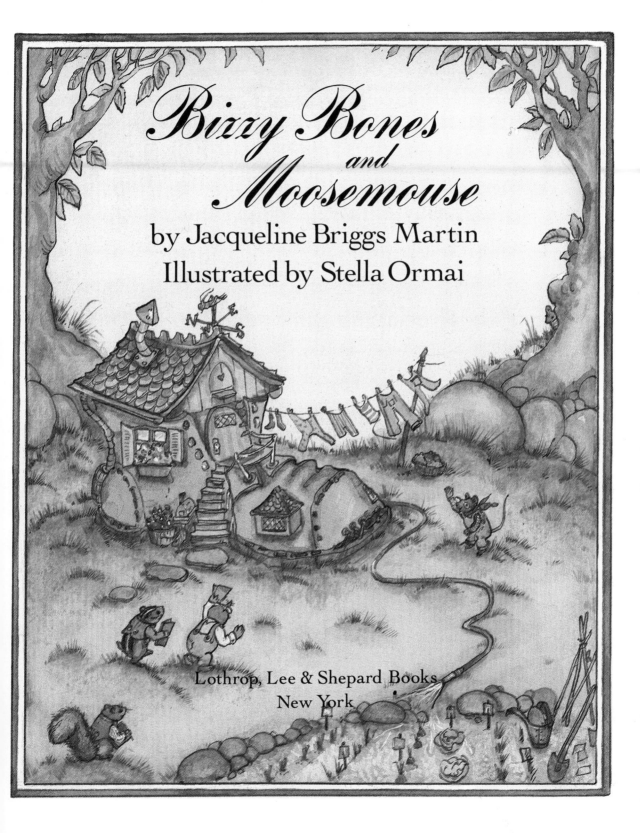

Bizzy Bones
and
Moosemouse

by Jacqueline Briggs Martin
Illustrated by Stella Ormai

Lothrop, Lee & Shepard Books
New York

First Edition   1 2 3 4 5 6 7 8 9 10

Library of Congress Cataloging in Publication Data
Martin, Jacqueline Briggs. Bizzy Bones and Moosemouse. Summary: Bizzy does not look forward
to his stay with big, loud Moosemouse when Uncle
Ezra goes away but the visit does not turn out as
expected. [1. Friendship—Fiction. 2. Animals—Fic-
tion] I. Ormai, Stella, ill. II. Title. PZ7.M363165Bf
1986 [E] 85-10950 ISBN 0-688-05745-4 ISBN 0-688-
05746-2 (lib. bdg.)

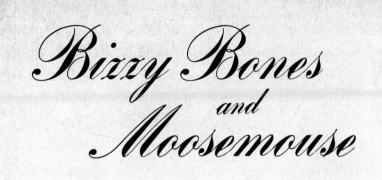

Bizzy Bones
and
Moosemouse

One summer, Uncle Ezra's card club
decided to take a trip to Paris Hill.
"We will leave after radish season,"
Uncle Ezra told Bizzy Bones.
"And I will be gone four days.
You can stay with Moosemouse."
"Moosemouse!" said Bizzy.
"I'd rather stay in a squash blossom."
"No," said Uncle Ezra.
"You'll be safe with Moosemouse."

So, after the last radish was pulled and eaten,
Bizzy packed his things and said goodbye
to his merry-go-round, his mailbox, and his bed.
As he followed Uncle Ezra through the Sweet Meadow
toward the edge of Piney Woods,
Bizzy counted butterflies
and tried not to think about Moosemouse.

But it was hard to forget that old fix-it.
Moosemouse lived beside a looming junk pile
in a dark, drafty tree trunk
that smelled like bugs and bad potatoes.
He didn't even have a bed—
just a pile of pine needles.

They found Moosemouse taking wheels off bicycles.
"Moosemouse can fix everything
from broken blossoms to bedsprings,"
Uncle Ezra always said.
Bizzy thought he just liked junk.

"Hello Frizzy, you old rhubarb," Moosemouse said,
lifting him high in the air.
Moosemouse always called Bizzy silly names
that made him feel like a baby.

Uncle Ezra gave Bizzy one giant hug
and said goodbye, leaving him alone with Moosemouse.
Bizzy wrapped himself up in his quilt
and thought about his empty work-shoe home
and Uncle Ezra, gone to Paris Hill.

The next morning, Bizzy pulled the quilt up over his head
when Moosemouse played the French horn.
Moosemouse knew one song—"The Wabash Cannonball."
He played it every morning,
as loud as screaming elephants.

Then Moosemouse made his best
pine powder pancakes for breakfast.
Bizzy couldn't eat them—
they weren't like Uncle Ezra's.

After breakfast, Moosemouse went outside
to bang away on a teapot.
Bizzy stayed inside and played with
Moosemouse's broken clocks.
In Moosemouse's dark tree trunk, every corner
and every bit of floor was piled high.
Bizzy saw a long-legged bug
crawl under one of those piles.
He was sure there were other bugs—probably bigger.
"I'll take the path into Piney Woods," Bizzy thought.
"Moosemouse won't care,
and I'll be back by suppertime."

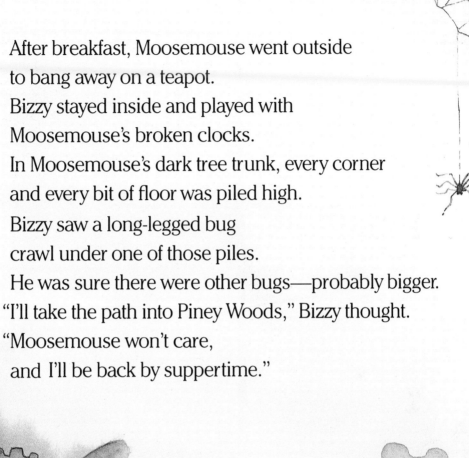

Deep in Piney Woods, Bizzy found
a pile of pine cones.
With them, he made a castle,
and he called himself Brave Bones.
He fought off pretend beasts of every sort
and won medals and card games, too.
Before long, the woods began to get dark.
Bizzy thought he heard an owl
and decided it was time to leave.

But now the trees all looked the same.
He couldn't find the path.
His castle didn't seem strong enough
to keep out real beasts,
and Bizzy felt very small.
He imagined Uncle Ezra saying,
"I never should have left my Bizzy
to be lost in those wild woods."

Then the rain started.
It pounded on Bizzy's head.
It dropped into his ears and dripped off his nose.
He fell into the mud and sat there—
too wet and heavy to get up.
He thought of Uncle Ezra and how sad he would be.
"Lost in the mud," he would say to Moosemouse.
"Lost and gone, and he was such a fine little mouse."
Suddenly, a huge noise gave Bizzy a chill.
It couldn't be elephants.
Perhaps it was thunder.

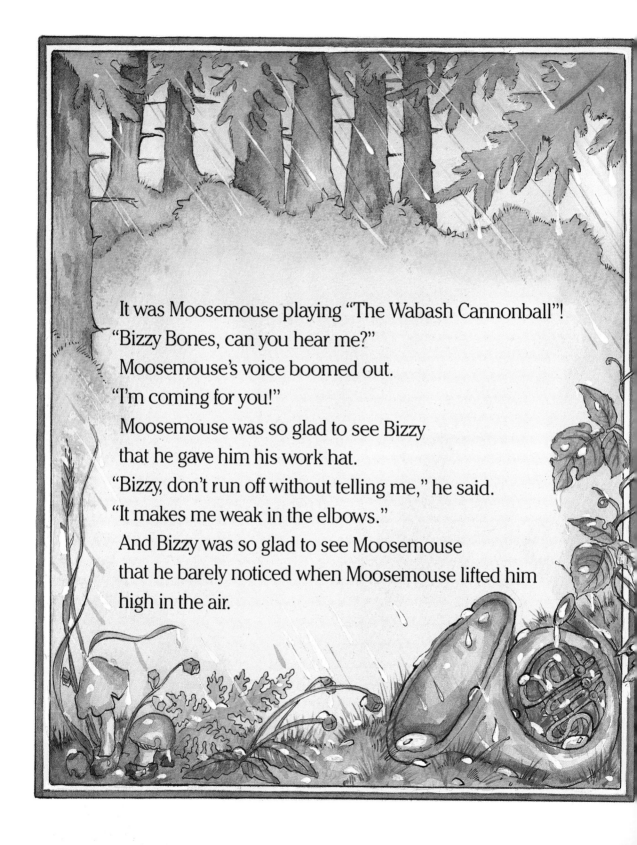

It was Moosemouse playing "The Wabash Cannonball"!
"Bizzy Bones, can you hear me?"
Moosemouse's voice boomed out.
"I'm coming for you!"
Moosemouse was so glad to see Bizzy
that he gave him his work hat.
"Bizzy, don't run off without telling me," he said.
"It makes me weak in the elbows."
And Bizzy was so glad to see Moosemouse
that he barely noticed when Moosemouse lifted him
high in the air.

Back in the tree trunk, they washed off the mud
in Moosemouse's shower.
Then Moosemouse gave Bizzy a cup of blossom tea
and tucked him into the pile of pine needles.

The next morning Bizzy felt hot and cold
at the same time.
He felt green.
He thought his bones were outside of his body,
and he wanted Uncle Ezra.
"You're sick from all that rain," said Moosemouse.
"Don't worry, I will take care of you."

Bizzy's head hurt.

"No yelling, no noise," he whispered.

"No noise," whispered Moosemouse.

He fixed Bizzy a bed from a cheesebox and a winter coat.

While Bizzy slept, Moosemouse tiptoed about
looking for this and that.

When Bizzy woke up, he could hear Moosemouse singing
low sweet songs about rovers and riverboat riders.

In the afternoon, Moosemouse brought Bizzy
a cool strawberry and a mint leaf.
He made buttercup soup—Bizzy's favorite—for supper.
Then he taught Bizzy a song about soup.
  Sarah Warah make a wish,
  Bring me soup in a dish.
  Take smiles, sharp cheese, a buttercup,
  Stir three times and serve it up.

The next morning Bizzy said,
"I feel as strong as you, Moosemouse,
and as quick as a chipmunk.
Let's fix something—a surprise for Uncle Ezra."
"We will be the surprise," Moosemouse said.
"We'll finish this six-seater,
pedal it to Paris Hill,
and give Uncle Ezra a ride home."
Bizzy had never seen anything like the six-seater.
The teapot, bicycle wheels, benches, and pillows
were somehow fitted together and wired tight.
Bizzy brought out a clock for the front seat.
Moosemouse fixed the steering wheel.

Then they pedaled across the Sweet Meadow,
past the Brambles, and into Paris Hill.

They found the card club
eating popcorn and playing cards
at the corner table of the Little-Cheeses Cracker Shop.
Uncle Ezra gave Bizzy a long hug
and a box with a lamp that burned for a year.
He let Bizzy hold the cards for a game of Spit-on-the-Cat.

Then they all climbed onto the six-seater and rode home.
Now Moosemouse keeps the cheesebox bed
in a special place in his tree trunk.
When the card club goes to Paris Hill
and Bizzy stays with Moosemouse,
he has his own corner.
The two mice fix things together and sing songs
about rovers and riverboat riders.

But Bizzy always remembers to take his light
to keep out the dark at Moosemouse's.
And he brings enough lunch for both of them.

PARIS
HILL

THE
BRAMBLES

TO BIZZY & EZRA
BONES' HOME